MW00484216

Black Boy Ballad

Martha Sylla Underwood

Illustration by Ananta Mohanta

Black Boy Ballad

www.playfulprose.com

ISBN 978-1-953653-10-9

First Edition

To my boys,
You were etched into my soul from the beginning.
Your eyes carry immeasurable depth of feeling and
your hearts are filled with divine and pure love. You
are both God's love ballad to earth.

- Mommy

When I lay down in my bed,
many worries creep in my head.

Is this how it's going to be?
People seeing my skin and hating me?

I sit still and quiet like Mom and Dad said,
to calm my spirit with love instead.

I close my eyes and try not to peek,
to hear God when he starts to speak.

My eyes got big, I wondered if it were true.
Is that really a heavenly voice coming through?

"Son, let me tell you all that you are.
You are my very special little star."

"Let me show you all the ways
you are royal and designed to amaze."

"Bold Black boy, you were made in my image, to grow big and strong, to protect the village."

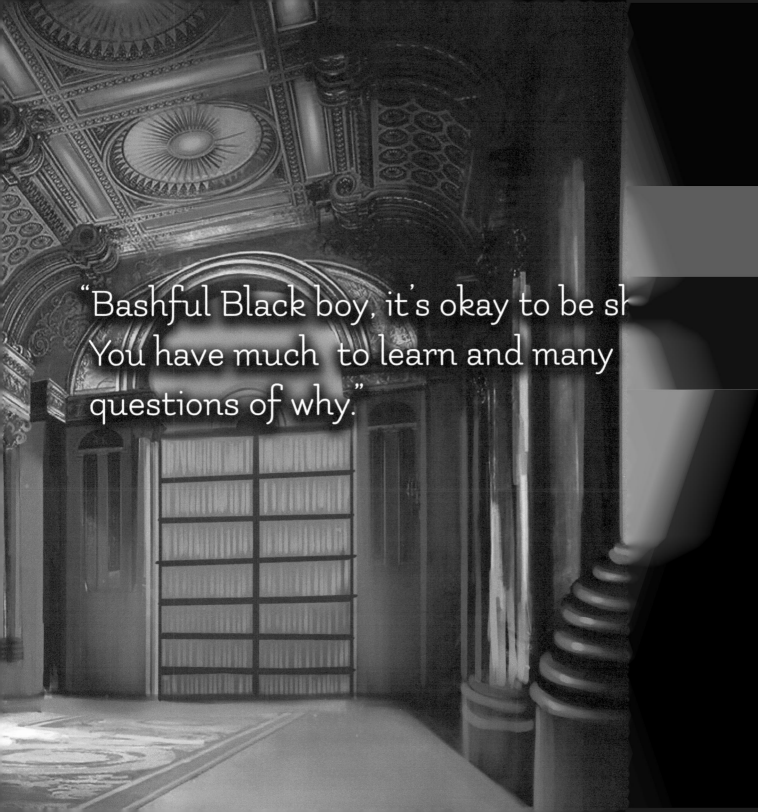

"Bashful Black boy, it's okay to be sh
You have much to learn and many
questions of why."

"Beaming Black boy, with smiles so bright,"

"don't let anyone dim your light!"

"Baffling Black boy, many will fail to understand"

"why I made you the first earthly man."

"Brave Black boy, despite the challenges you face,"

"Brilliant Black boy, all will marvel at your smarts.
You master science, technology, and even the arts."

"Beautiful Black boy, you are my gift to mankind.
Don't ever take for granted your mastermind!"

"Black Boy King, my love ballad to earth, never ever, forget your eternal worth."

The End

CPSIA information can be obtained
at www.ICGtesting.com
Printed in the USA
BVHW020414151121
621673BV00006B/433